5-Minute Maisy Stories

Lucy Cousins

Candlewick Press

Contents

Maisy's Morning on the Farm

Maisy wakes
up early.

There's plenty
of work to do
on the farm.

First Maisy feeds
the chickens.

She fills her bucket
with corn.

Here, chickens!
Come and have
your breakfast.

Next Maisy
feeds the pigs.
They're hungry!

The sheep have lots of tasty grass to eat.

It's time to milk
the cow. Moo!

Squish squish,
squirt squirt.
Maisy fills the
bucket with milk.

Now it's time
for breakfast.
Maisy puts
cereal and milk
in her bowl.

Little Black Cat
wants milk, too.

Good work, Maisy!
Have a great day!

Maisy Goes Shopping

Maisy is visiting
Charley today.

Hello, Charley.
Hello, Maisy.

It's almost time
for lunch, but
Charley's fridge
is empty.

Let's go shopping!

Maisy chooses some apples and bananas.

Mmmm, they look good.

Charley gets
some juice.

What else do
they need?

Bread, tomatoes, cheese, and yogurt.

That's everything.

Now it's time to pay.

Look at all that food!

It's a good thing Maisy brought her wagon.

Maisy and Charley
unpack the bags.

Then at last . . .

. . . they have some lunch.
Hooray!

Maisy Dresses Up

Maisy has been invited to Tallulah's costume party.

What will Maisy be?

She looks in her dress-up box.

She could be
a pirate.
But Charley is
already dressed
up as a pirate.

She could be
a queen.
But Eddie is
already dressed
up as a king.

She could be
a firefighter.
But Cyril is already
dressed up as a
firefighter.

Maisy has a good idea! She will make her own special costume.

Charley, Eddie,
and Cyril are
already at
Tallulah's house
when . . .

. . . the doorbell rings. In comes a zebra.

Oh, it's Maisy!

Hello, everyone.
It's party time!

Maisy Makes Lemonade

It's a hot day.
Maisy is having
a nice cold drink.

Mmmm. Lemonade.

Eddie is hot, too.
Maisy shares
the lemonade

Eddie takes a big
drink . . .

. . . and it's all gone!

Poor Eddie.

He is very thirsty.

Maisy has an idea.

She goes to
the lemon tree in
the garden.

She picks some fruit—with a little help from Eddie!

In the kitchen,
Eddie squeezes lemon
juice into a pitcher.

Maisy adds
water.

Then Eddie stirs in some sugar. There! A fresh pitcher of delicious lemonade.

Maisy goes to
get the cups.

Slurp!

What's that noise?

It's Eddie!
He couldn't wait.

But there's plenty
for Maisy, too.
Good job!

Maisy Cleans Up

Maisy is cleaning her house today.

Ding-dong!

Someone is at the door. Who could it be?

It's Charley!

He's come for
a visit.

He can help
Maisy clean!

Charley smells
something delicious
in the kitchen.

He's hungry.

Oh, look—cupcakes!
But the floor
is still wet.
Charley has to wait
until it's dry.

While he's waiting,
Charley puts the
toys away.

Maisy vacuums
the living room.

Then Charley washes the windows from the inside . . .

. . . and Maisy washes them from the outside.

That looks better!

At last the kitchen floor is dry.

Now Maisy and Charley can have some cupcakes.

Hooray!

Good job, Maisy.
Good job, Charley.
Treats! Yum, yum!

Maisy Takes a Bath

It's Maisy's bathtime.

She runs the water and puts in some bubbles . . .

. . . and in goes Duck.

Ding-dong!
Oh, that's
the doorbell.

Maisy runs
downstairs to
see who it is.

Hello, Tallulah.

Maisy can't play now. It's her bathtime.

Maisy runs back upstairs and gets undressed.

Maisy jumps into
the bubbly bath.

Ding-dong!
Who is ringing the
doorbell now?

Hello again, Tallulah!

Maisy is still taking her bath. Come and play later.

Oh! Where are you going, Tallulah?

Tallulah runs up
to the bathroom
and takes off
her clothes.

Splash, splash!

Maisy and Tallulah play in the bath.

Hooray!

Maisy's Bedtime

Maisy is sleepy.
It's time for bed.
It's bedtime for
Panda, too.

Maisy closes her bedroom curtains.

Tuwhoo, tuwhoo, hoots the owl.

Maisy washes her face and brushes her teeth.

Maisy puts on
her pajamas.

Maisy gets
into bed and
reads a story.

But where
is Panda?

Is he in the
toy box?

Oh, there he is!

Maisy turns
off the light.

But she still
isn't ready to
go to sleep.

Maisy forgot to
use the toilet!

Panda sits on
his potty, too.

Maisy is very
sleepy now.

Good night, Maisy.
Good night, Panda.